SCOOBY-DOO!

MONSTER Jokes!

by Michael Dahl
illustrated by Scott Jeralds

Stone Arch Books
A Capstone Imprint

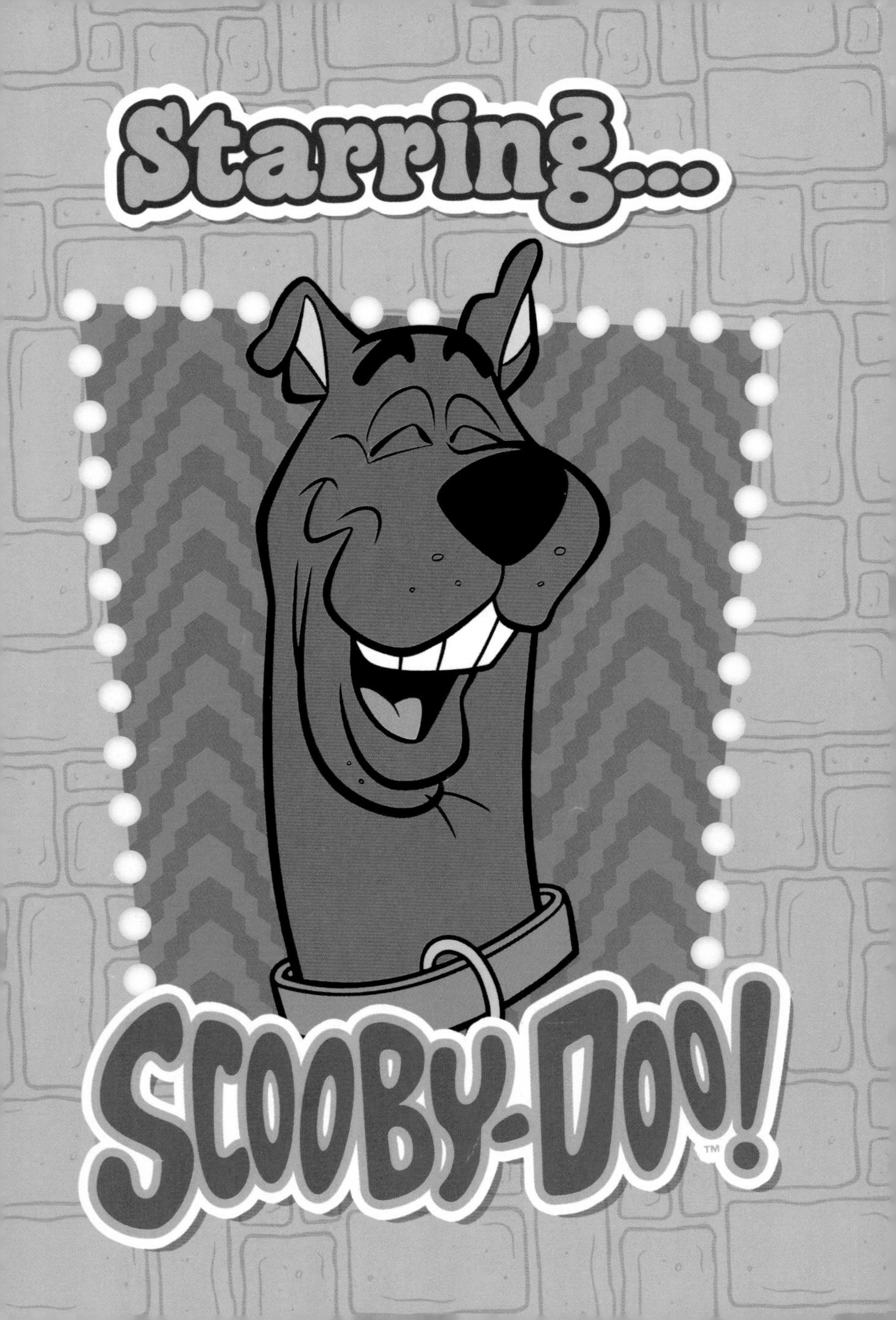
Starring...
SCOOBY-DOO!™

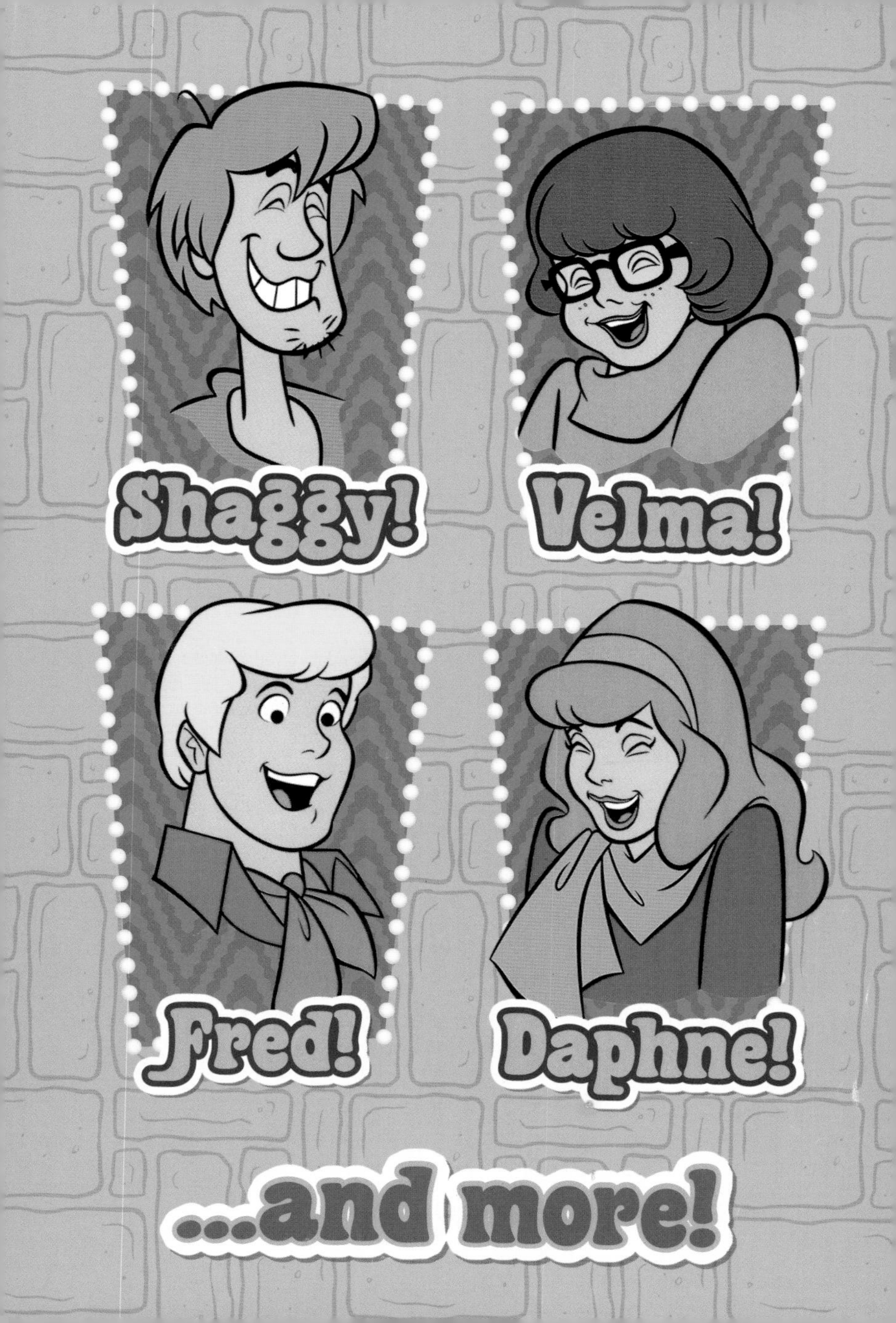

Shaggy!
Velma!
Fred!
Daphne!
...and more!

Scooby-Doo Joke Books
are published by Stone Arch Books,
A Capstone Imprint
1710 Roe Crest Drive
North Mankato, Minnesota 56003
www.capstonepub.com

CAPS33427

Cataloging-in-Publication Data is available on the Library of Congress website.
ISBN: 978-1-4342-9681-8 [Library Hardcover]
ISBN: 978-1-4965-0198-1 [eBook PDF]

Summary:
Who says monsters can't be funny? Scooby-Doo and friends are ready to make you
laugh out loud with some of the scariest monsters we know!

Editor: Eliza Leahy
Designer: Bob Lentz
Production: Gene Bentdahl

Printed in China by Nordica
0914/CA21401506
092014   008470NORDS15

Set List:

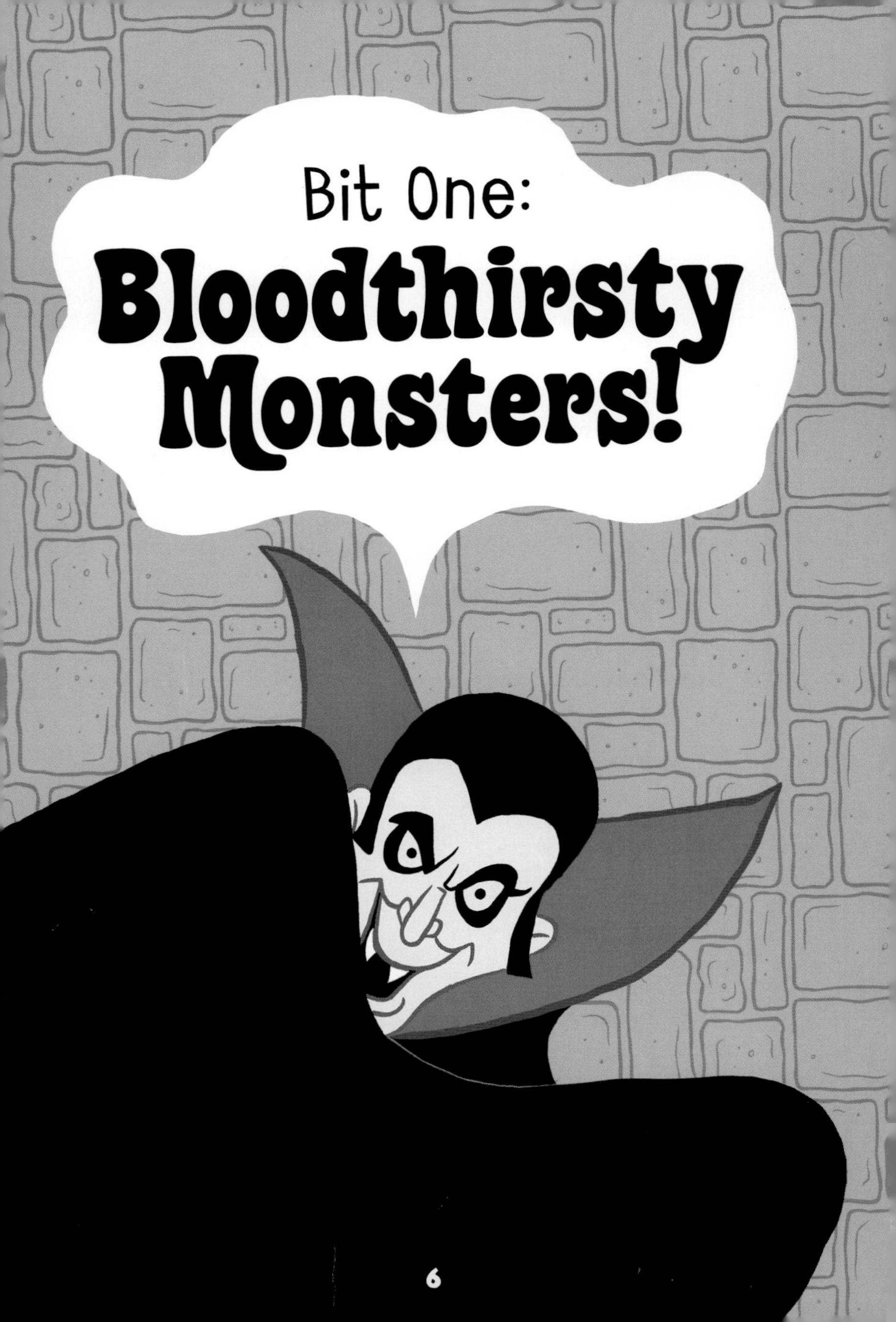
Bit One:
Bloodthirsty Monsters!

What's the best way to help a starving zombie?
Give him a hand!

When do zombies go to sleep?
Only when they're dead tired.

What do zombies like eating the most in a restaurant?

The waiters!

Where's the safest place in your house to hide from zombies?
The *living* room, of course.

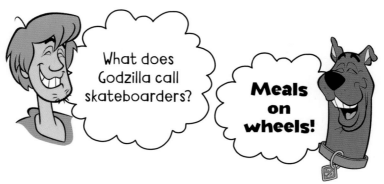

What does Godzilla call skateboarders?

Meals on wheels!

Why is Godzilla so good at sneaking up on people?
He's a crept-tile.

What did Godzilla say when he saw a rush-hour train full of passengers?
"Chew-chew!"

What's the best way to speak to Godzilla?
Long distance!

Why did Godzilla eat all the furniture in the hotel room?
He had a suite tooth!

Did you hear that Godzilla got sick and threw up?
Yeah, it's all over town!

What do you call Godzilla in a phone booth?

Stuck!

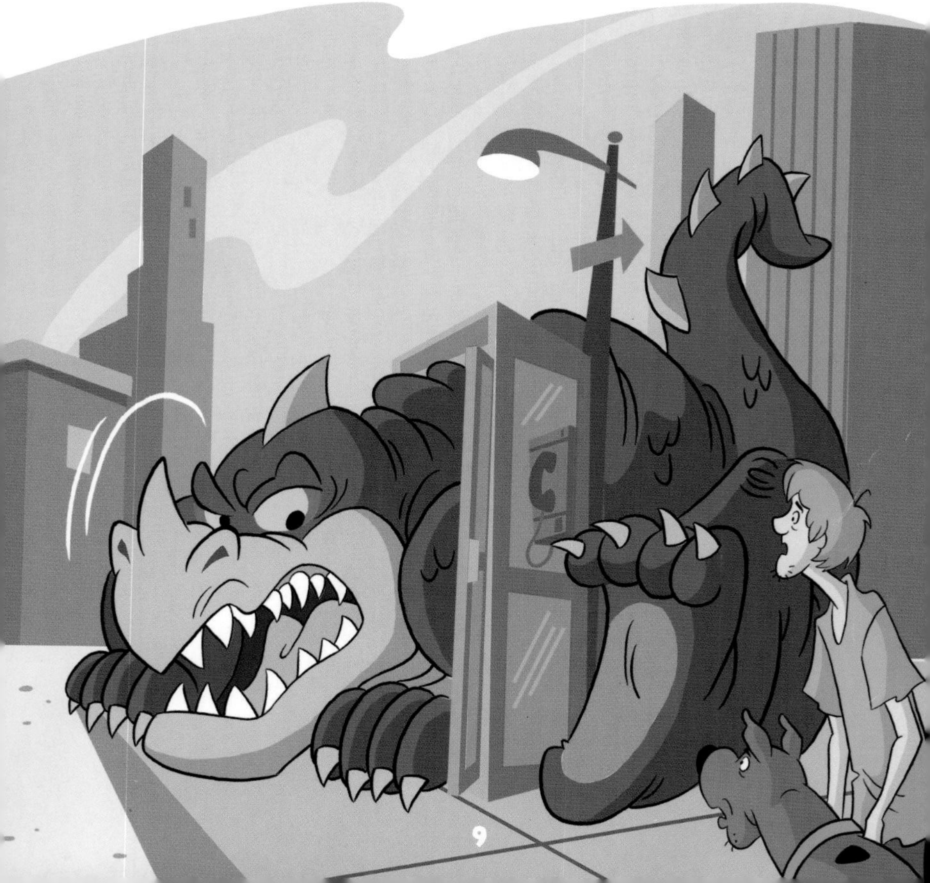

How does Dracula like his coffee?
De-coffin-ated!

When did Dracula realize that sunlight could destroy him?

When it finally *dawned* on him!

What kind of dog does Dracula have?
A bloodhound!

Why won't anyone kiss Dracula?
He has *bat* breath!

Why was the vampire studying all night long?
She was getting ready for her blood test!

What do you say to a vampire who wants to go on a date?
"Fangs, but no fangs!"

Why don't vampires have many friends?

They're such pains in the neck!

What's a vampire's favorite fruit?
Neck-tarines.

Why did the zombie lose the card game?

He had a rotten hand!

What do you call a zombie door-to-door salesman?

A dead-ringer!

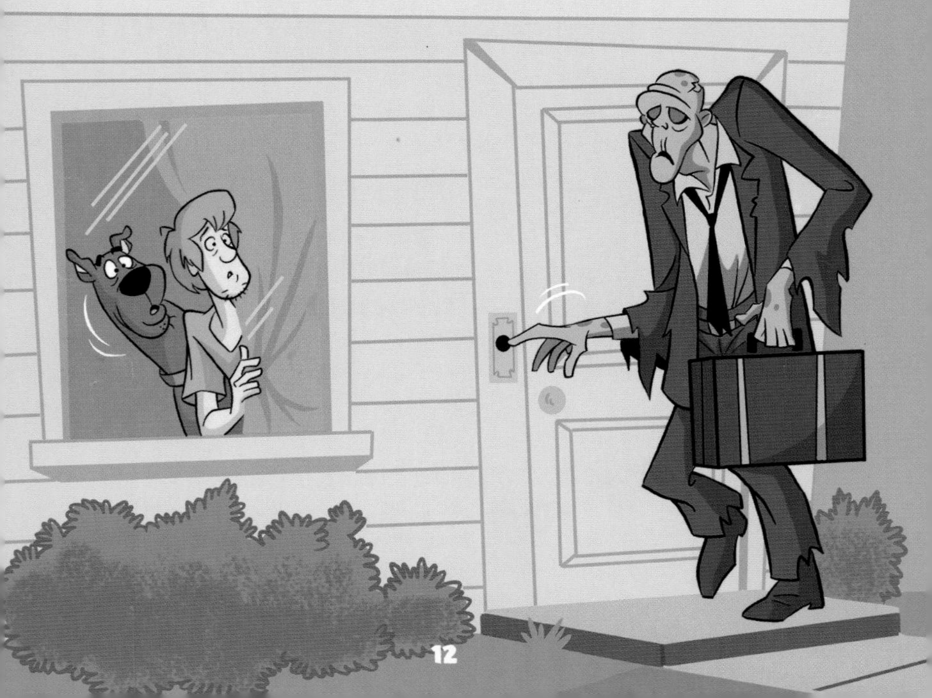

What happened when the zombie was late for the dinner party?
They gave him the cold shoulder.

What do you call a teenage zombie with no legs?
Grounded.

What did the zombie do when she lost her hand?
She went to the *secondhand* store!

What did the little zombie make of his new friends at school?
A pie!

What did the zombie eat after the dentist pulled out all his teeth?
The dentist!

Don't make a vampire angry. **They have very *bat* tempers!**

What does Dracula take when he has a cold?
Coffin medicine!

What do goblins like to put on their bagels?
Scream cheese!

That vampire sure is popular.

Yeah, she has a big fang club.

How did the vampire cure his sore throat?
He spent all day gargoyling!

Did you hear that a vampire attacked Sir Lancelot?

Yeah, he got a bite in shining armor!

What do little vampires eat for lunch?
Alpha-bat soup.

Where does Dracula keep his money?
In a blood bank.

Why don't vampires ever race each other?
They're always neck and neck!

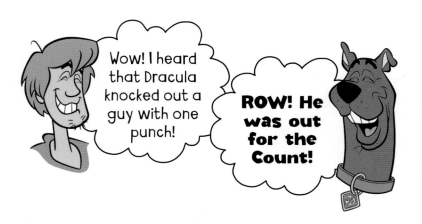

Wow! I heard that Dracula knocked out a guy with one punch!

ROW! He was out for the Count!

Did you know there's a vampire duck?
Of course. It's Count Quackula!

Why did the vampire flunk out of art class?
She could only *draw blood!*

I heard the new restaurant has a vampire for a chef.
Yes, he's Count Spatula!

What do you get if you cross
the Mystery Machine with a
bloodsucker?

A van-pire!

Bit Two:

Phantoms, Spirits, and Spooks!

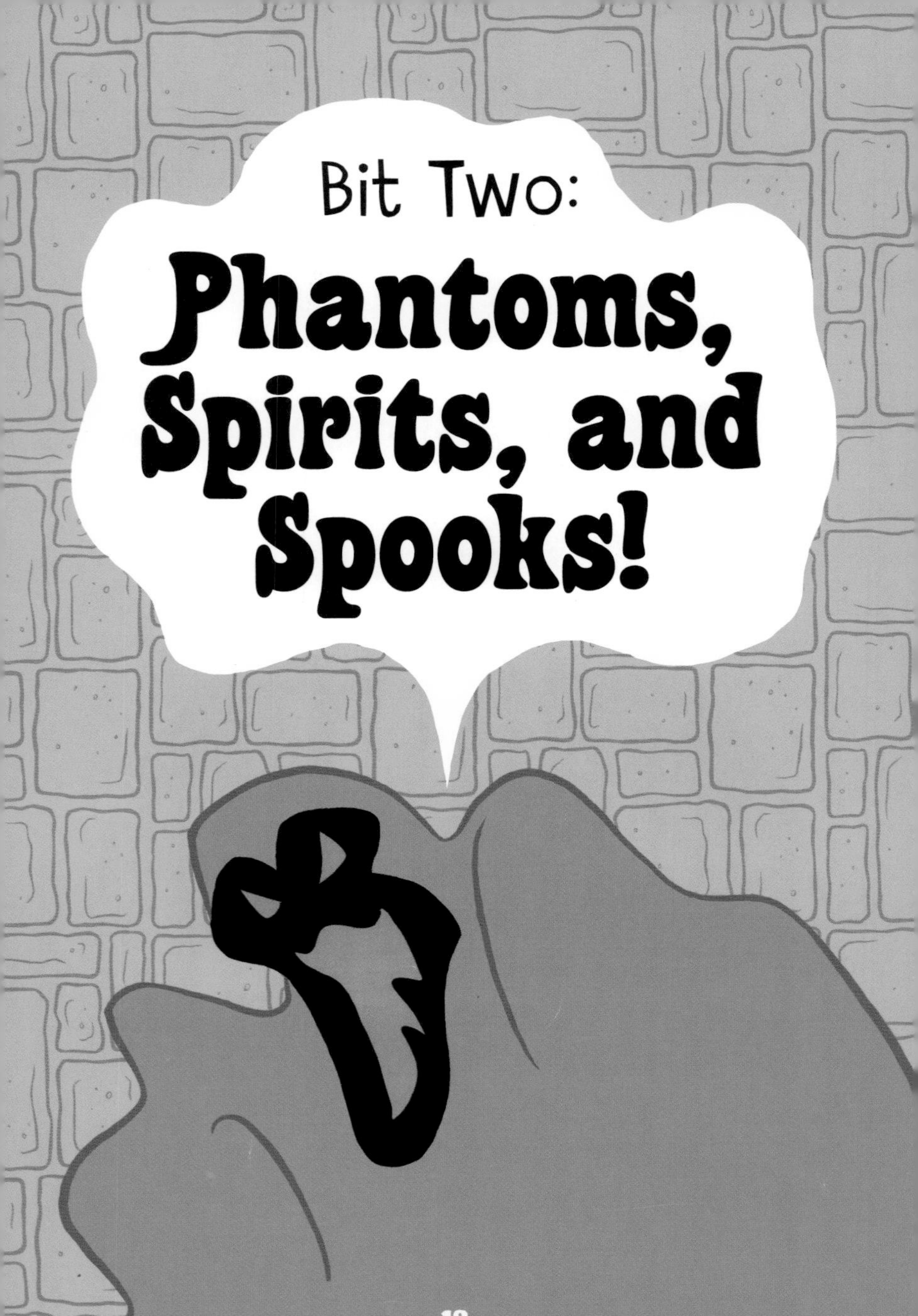

What do you call a ghost's mom and dad?
Trans-parents!

What do you call a haunted chicken?
A poultry-geist!

What keeps a ghost cool in the summer?
The scare conditioner.

What did the ghost wear to the fancy dinner?
A boo tie!

In what position do ghosts sleep?
Horror-zontal!

Where do ghosts go for treats?
The I-scream parlor!

What's a phantom's favorite game?
Hide-and-ghost-seek!

What do you say to a ghost when you meet one?
"How do you boo?"

What do baby ghosts wear on their feet?
Boo-ties!

Did you hear that
Dr. Frankenstein combined a
cocker spaniel, a poodle,
and a ghost?

Yup, he ended up with a cocker-poodle-boo!

When do ghosts wake up?

In the moaning!

What do teenage ghosts wear?
Boo jeans.

What's the first thing ghosts do when they get in a car?
Put on their sheet belts!

Why are ghosts so bad at telling lies?
You can always see right through them.

How do ghosts like their eggs for breakfast?

Terror-fried!

Why do ghosts like riding in elevators?

It raises their spirits!

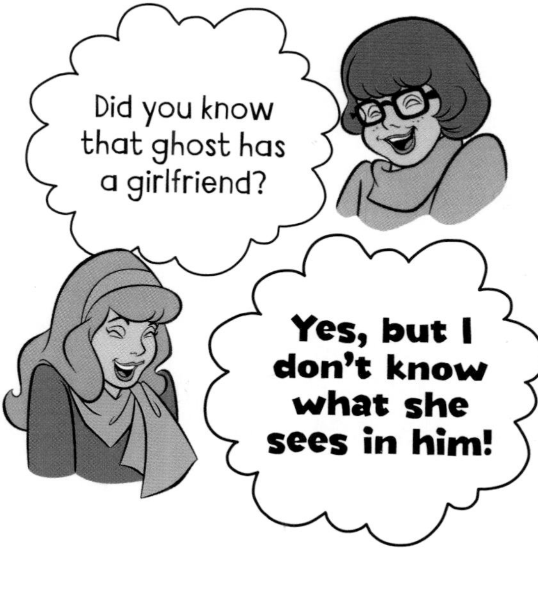
Did you know that ghost has a girlfriend?
Yes, but I don't know what she sees in him!

Bit Three:

Mad Scientist Jokes!

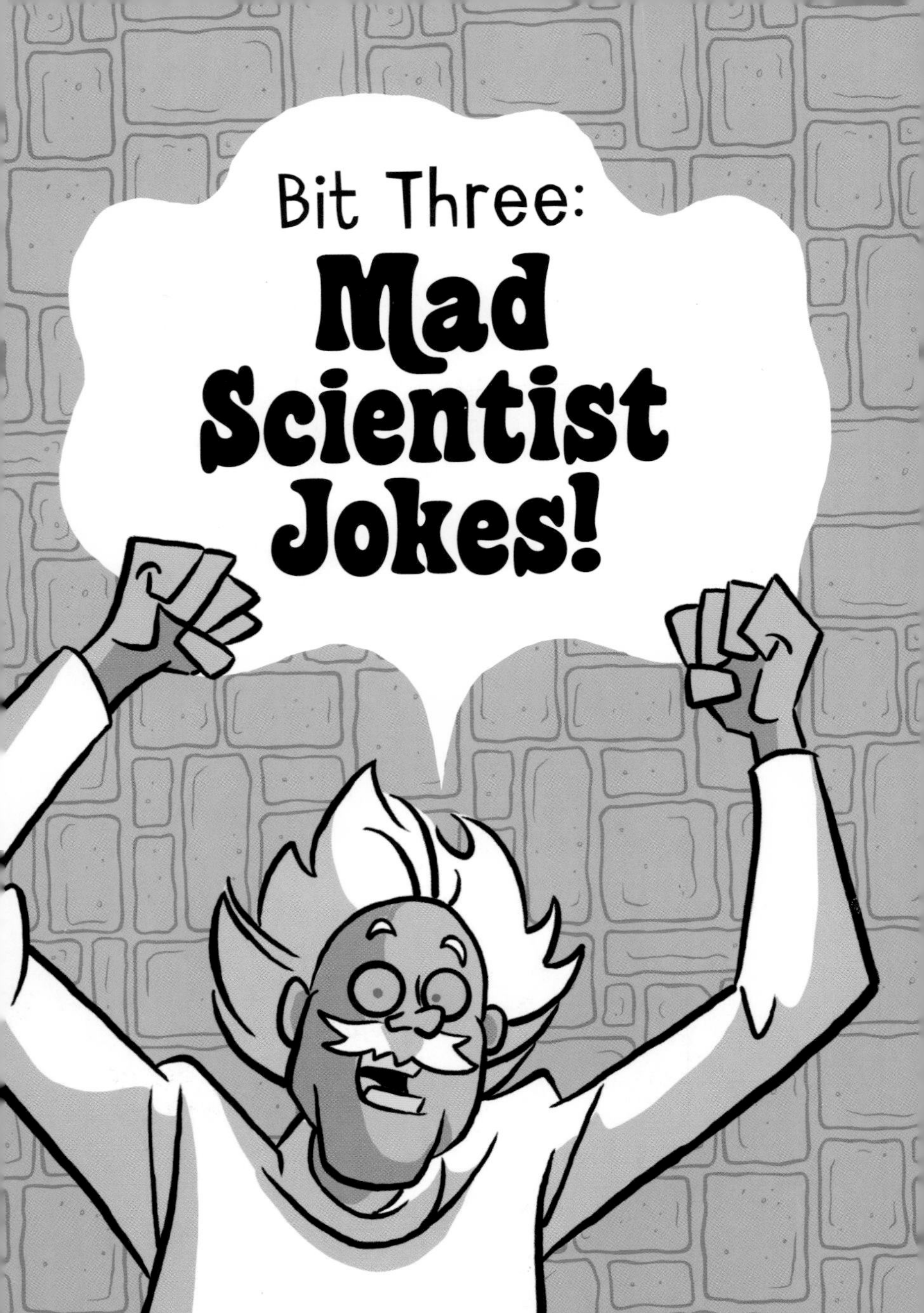

What happened to the mad scientist who crossed a pig with a grizzly?
He got a teddy boar!

What happened to the mad scientist who crossed a UFO with a wizard?
He got a flying sorcerer!

What happened to the mad scientist who crossed a slab of cheese with Frankenstein?
He got a really scary Muenster!

What happened to the
mad scientist who crossed
a snake with a Lego set?
**He got a
boa constructor!**

What happened to
the mad scientist who
crossed a turtle with a
porcupine?
**He got a
slowpoke.**

What happened to
the mad scientist who
crossed a toad with a
distant galaxy?
**He got star
warts!**

What happened to the mad scientist who crossed a bear cub with a skunk?

He got Winnie the Phew!

What happened to the mad scientist who crossed a newborn snake with a trampoline?

He got a bouncing baby boa!

What happened to the mad scientist who crossed an alligator with a bunny?

He had to get a new bunny!

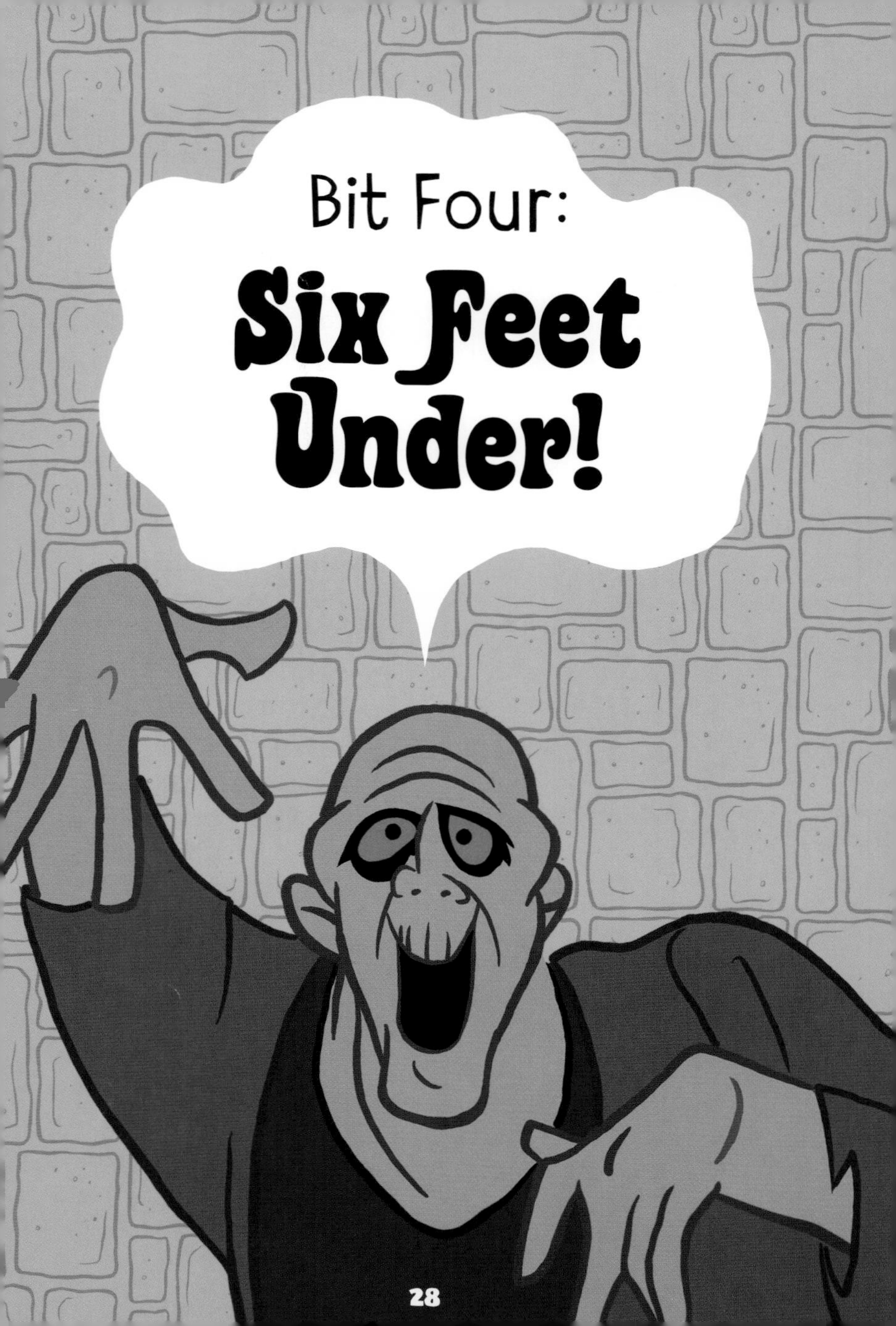
Bit Four:
Six Feet Under!

Why didn't the skeleton go to the school dance?
He had no *body* to go with!

Why was the skeleton so afraid of heights?
She just didn't have the guts!

Why did the skeleton keep his head in the freezer?
I guess he was a numbskull!

Why didn't the skeleton eat the cafeteria food?
He didn't have the stomach for it.

Where do skeletons go for vacation?
The Dead Sea!

Where can you always find a cemetery?
In the dead center of town.

What did the movie director say when she had
finished her mummy movie?
"That's a wrap!"

The doctor told the mummy he has the heart of a
much younger man.
**Yes, and the doctor told him he had
to give it back, too!**

Did you know that skeletons love riding motorcycles?
Yup, they're _bone_ to be wild!

What do skeletons order at restaurants?

Spare ribs!

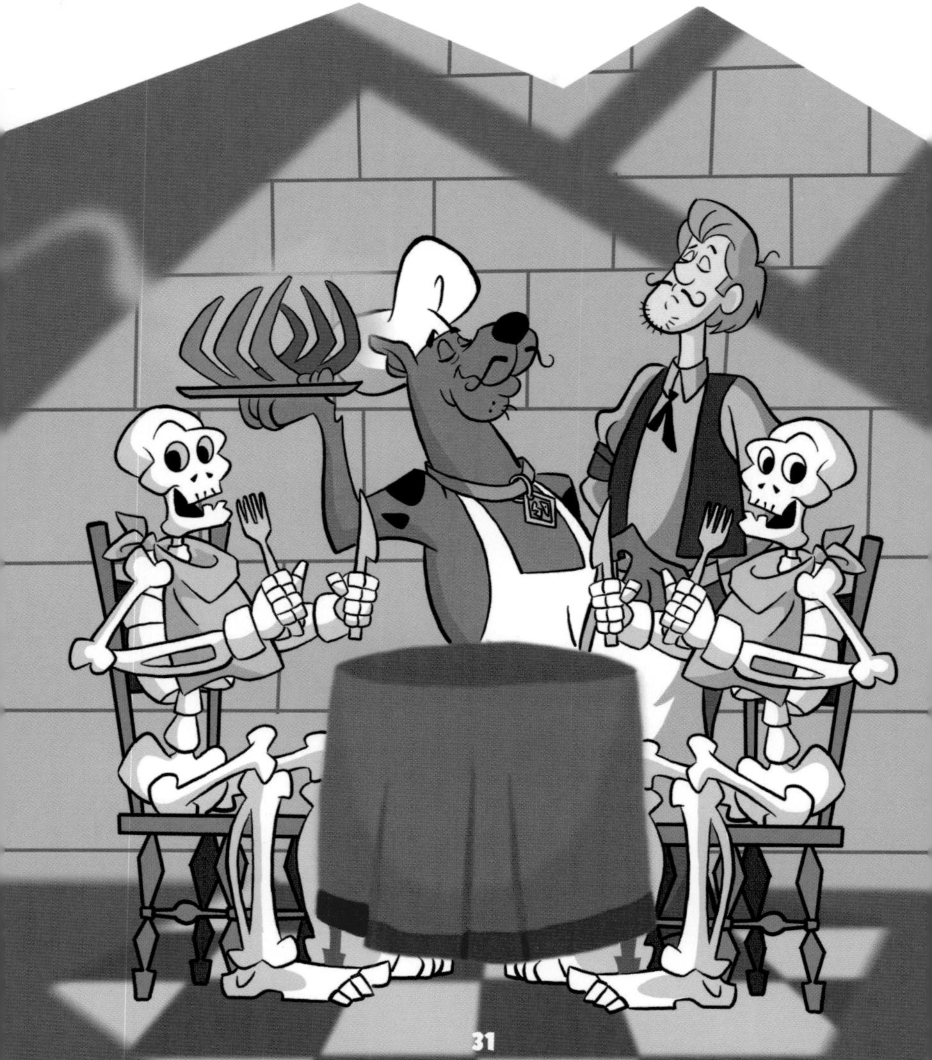

What did the father skeleton
say to his son who stayed in
bed all day?

"Lazy bones!"

Why doesn't the mummy have any friends?
She's too *wrapped up* in herself!

What did the ghoul say to his ghoulfriend?
"I really dig you!"

What does a skeleton say before every meal?
"Bone appétit!"

Who won the skeleton beauty contest?
No body!

Cemeteries are having a hard time finding room for all their guests.

Yes, it's a *grave* problem!

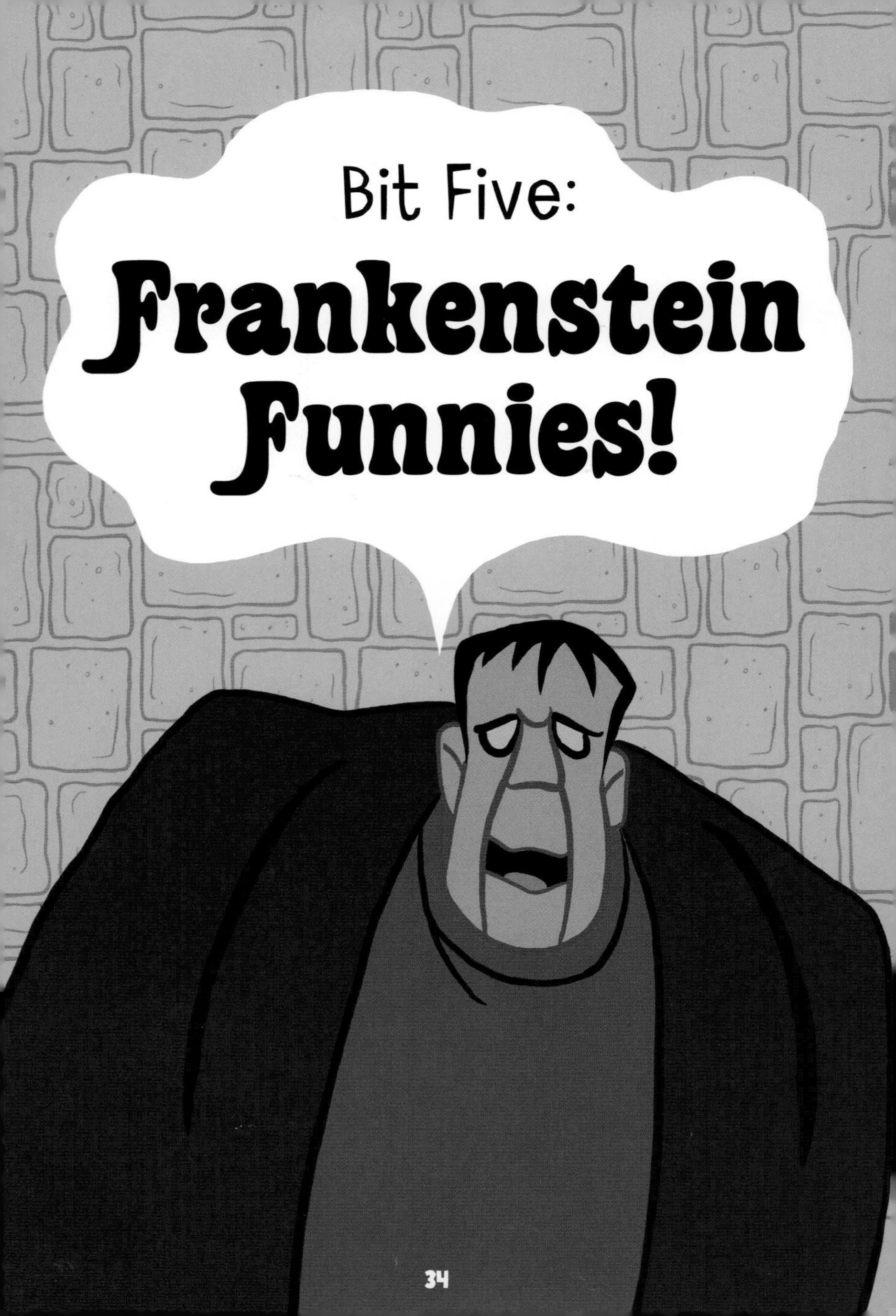
Bit Five:
Frankenstein Funnies!

Why did Frankenstein go to the psychiatrist?
He thought he had a screw loose!

Why did Frankenstein go to the restaurant
with a raisin?
He couldn't find a date!

What's Frankenstein's favorite dessert?
I scream!!!

Do you know where Frankenstein lives?
Sure, he's on a dead end.

I heard Dr. Frankenstein is a funny guy.

Yeah, he always keeps you in *stitches*!

Why is Dr. Frankenstein so popular?

He's very good at making friends.

Who is the world's smartest monster?
Frank-Einstein!

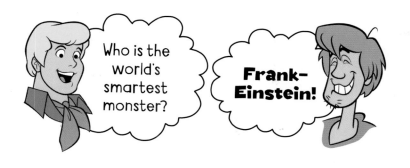

What did one of Frankenstein's ears say to the other?

"I didn't know we lived on the same block!"

What does it say on Frankenstein's gravestone?

"Rest in Pieces."

How did Frankenstein get rid of his headache?

He put his head through the window and the pane just disappeared!

What did Frankenstein say to the screwdriver?

"Daddy!"

Bit Six: Witch Is Witch?!

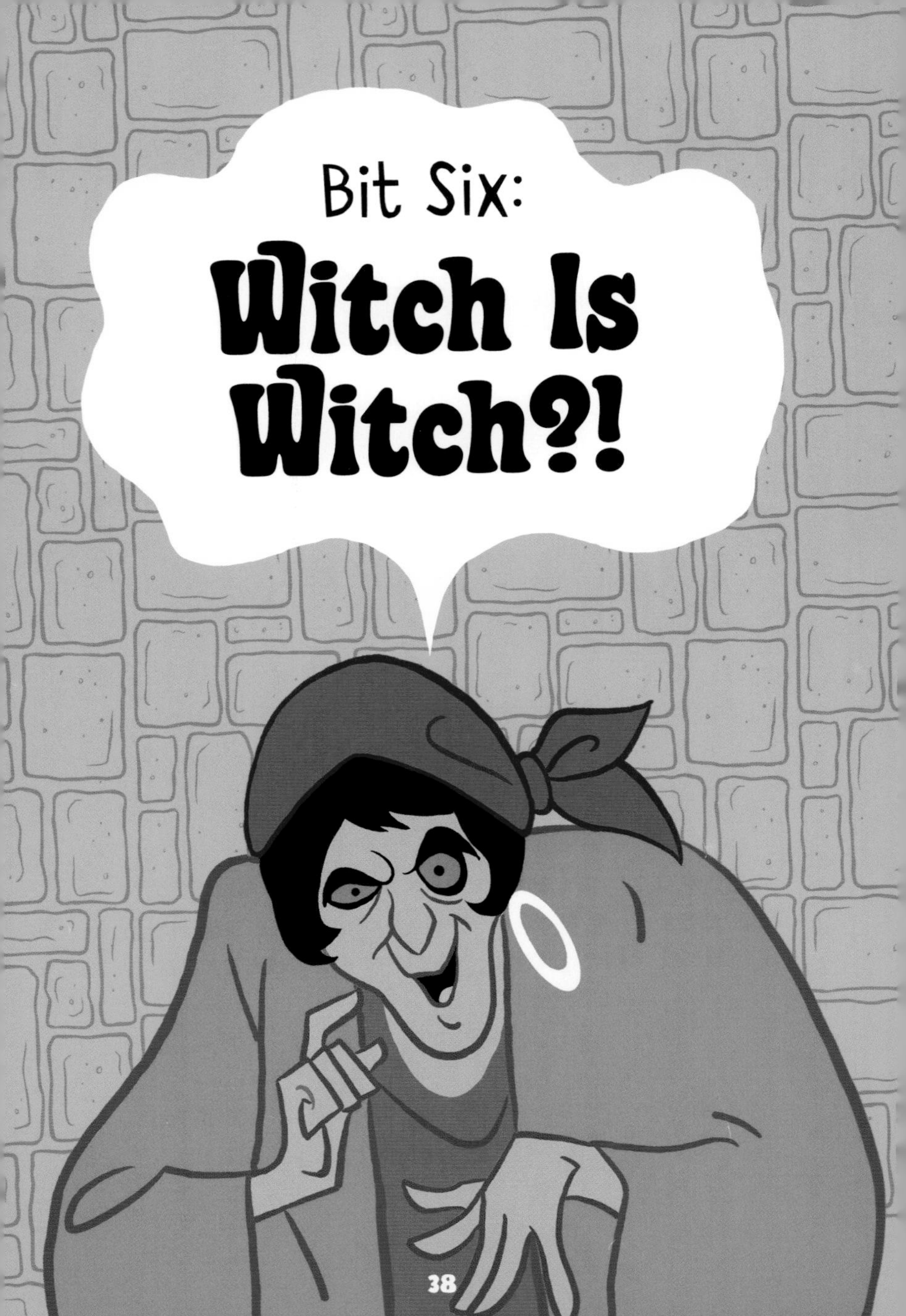

What do you call witches who live in the same room?
Broom-mates!

What do you call a nervous witch?
A twitch!

Watch out! We're being chased by twin sorceresses!
I know! I can't tell witch is witch!

Why was the witch late for the party?
Her broom overswept.

What did the sorceress have for a snack?

A sand-witch!

How does a wizard tell time?
With a witch-watch!

What do you get when you cross a witch's cat with a lemon?
A sourpuss.

Did you know that witches fall from the sky?
Yeah, and the angry ones fly off the handle!

What happened to the sorcerer who was thrown out of school?

He was ex-*spelled!*

What kind of sorceress is always helpful in the dark?

A lights-witch!

Bit Seven:

Prison Break!

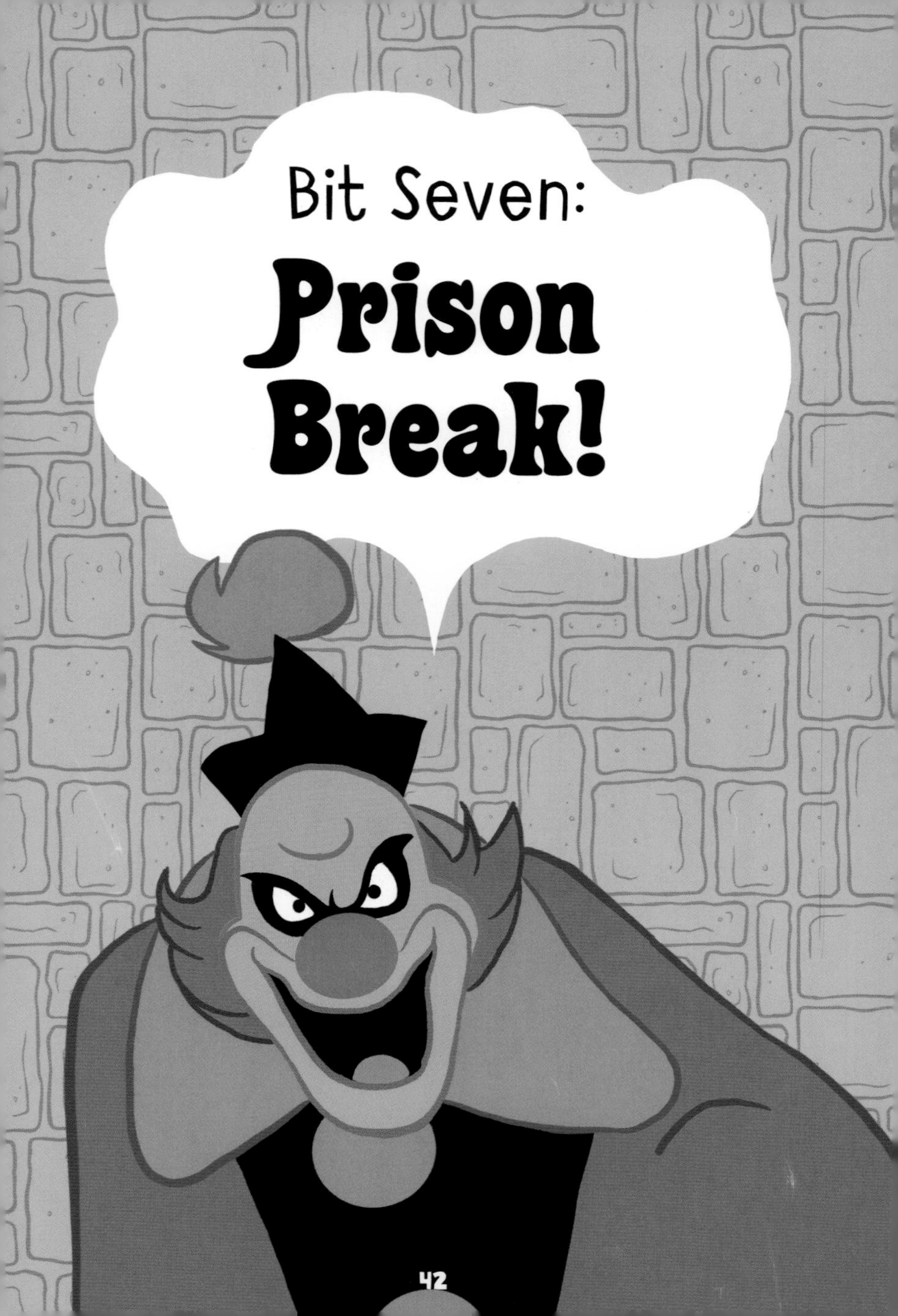

What happened when the giant brick monster escaped from prison?

They set up a road block!

What happened when the Human Fly
escaped from prison?
They brought in a SWAT team!

What happened when the Cyclops escaped from prison?

The police had to keep an eye open!

What happened when the evil hairstylist escaped from prison?

Police had to comb the area!

What happened when the mutant corn monster escaped from prison?

They called out the cobs!

What happened when a gang of monsters escaped through the sewers?

The police said it was a grime wave!

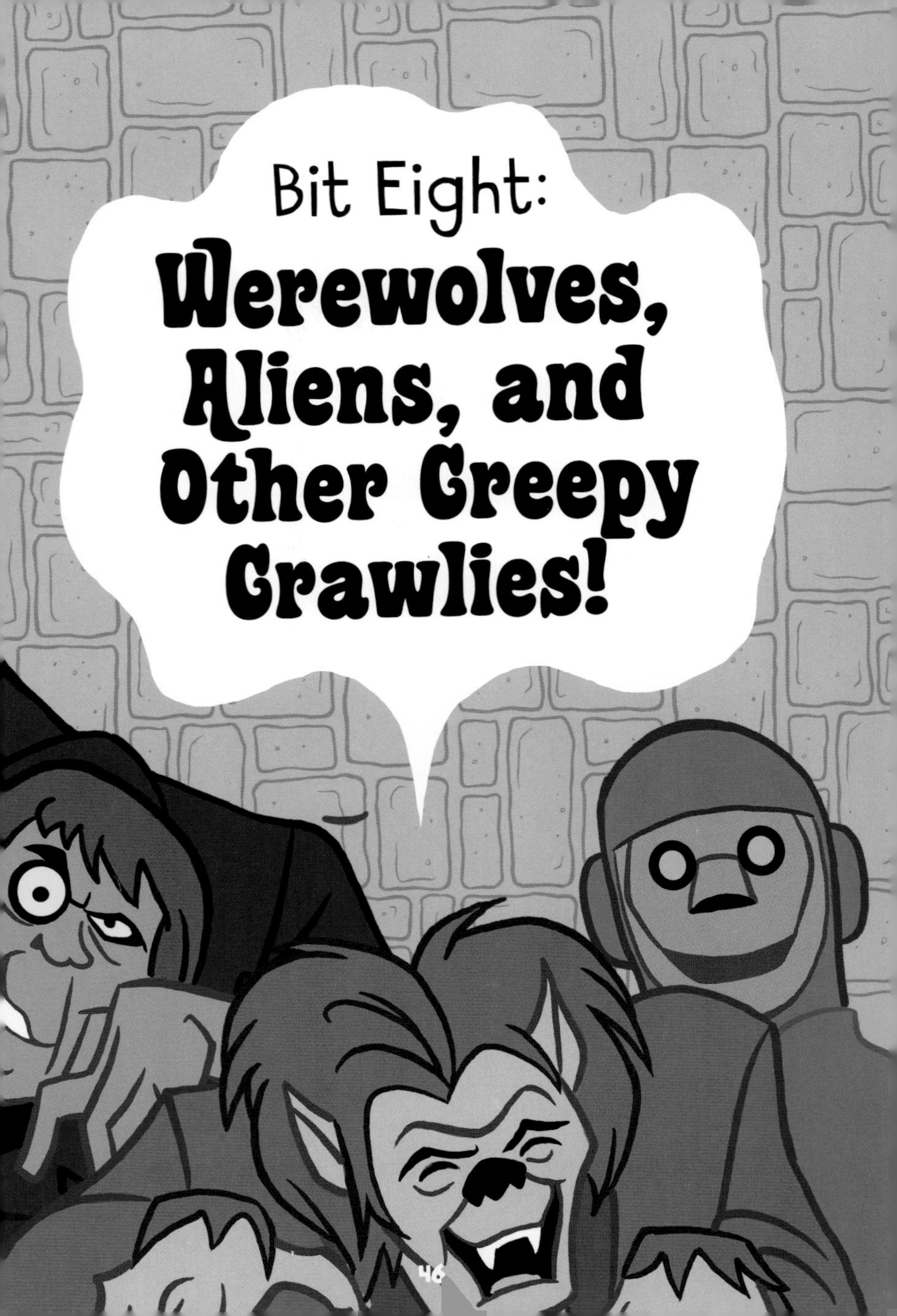
Bit Eight:
Werewolves, Aliens, and Other Creepy Crawlies!

Why didn't the monster ever go out with his friends after school?

He wasn't allowed to play with his food!

How many parents does a werewolf have?

Five. One ma and four paws.

What does a techno-nerdy pirate wear?

An iPatch.

What should you do if you're attacked by a gang of clowns?

Go for the juggler!

Where did the alien leave her UFO?

At a parking meteor.

What monster eats the fastest?
A goblin!

What planet did the evil aliens crash land on?
Splaturn!

What technique do aliens use for fighting?
Martian arts!

Why do dragons sleep during the day?
So they can fight knights!

Who's the center of attention at a monster dance party?

The boogie man!

What hand should you use to pet King Kong?

Someone else's!

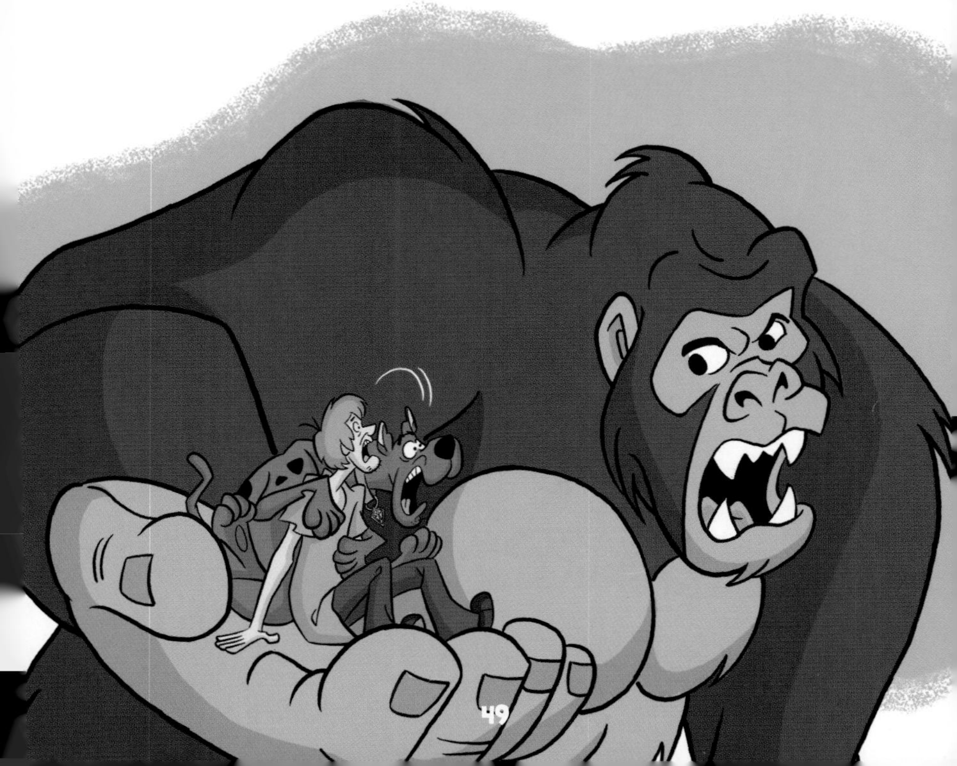

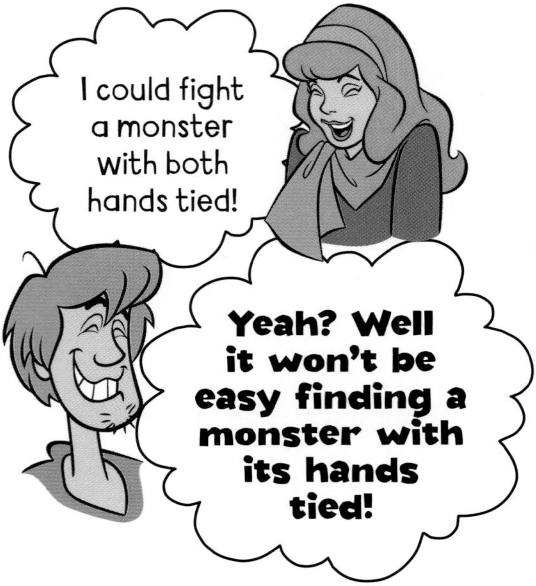
I could fight a monster with both hands tied!
Yeah? Well it won't be easy finding a monster with its hands tied!

How can you tell if there's a monster under your bed?

Your nose touches the ceiling!

What did Godzilla say after he caused the earthquake?

"Sorry, my fault!"

What do sea monsters like to eat?

Fish and ships!

Why did the headless horseman go to college?
He wanted to get *a head* in life!

Why did the monster's grandma knit him a new sock?
She heard that he grew another foot!

How do you mend a broken jack-o'-lantern?
With a pumpkin patch!

Why did King Kong climb the Empire State Building?

He was too big to use the stairs!

What do you call a one-eyed monster on a motorbike?

A Cycle-ops!

How can I contact the Loch Ness sea monster?

Drop it a line!

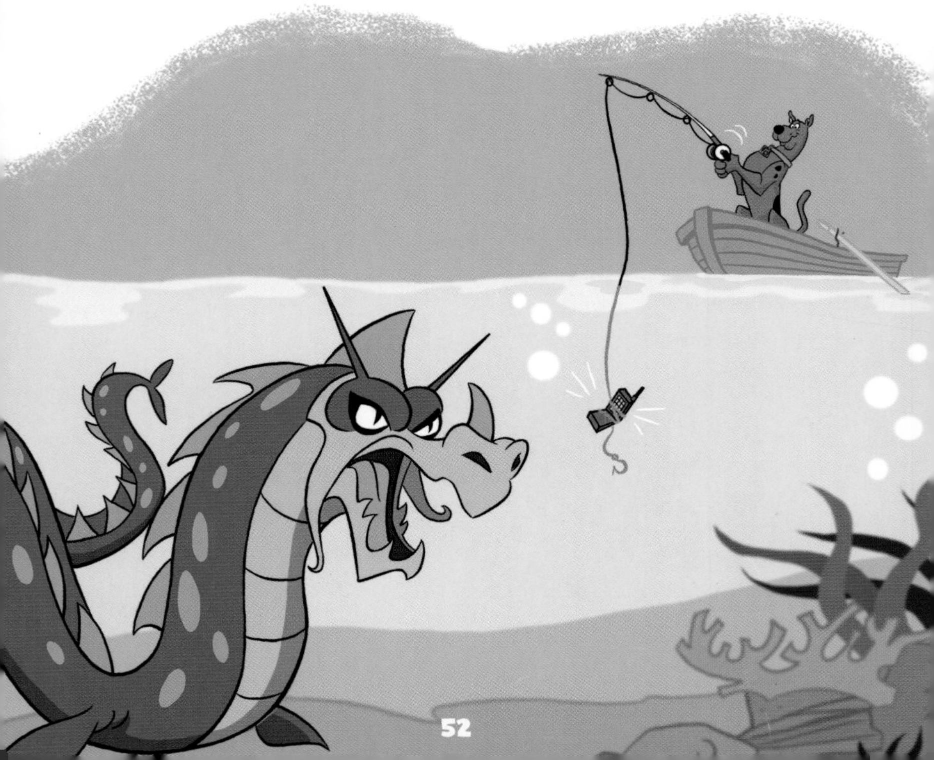

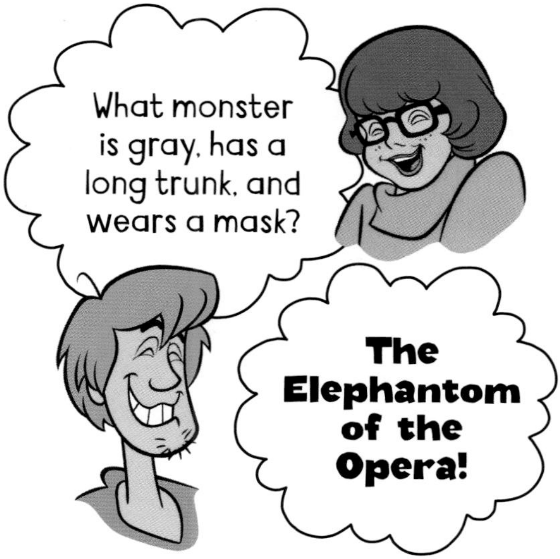
What monster is gray, has a long trunk, and wears a mask?
The Elephantom of the Opera!

Why is a graveyard a great place to write a book?

It's full of plots!

Where does the yeti keep his money?

In a snow bank.

What would you say if you saw three Cyclopes in a dark alley?

"Eye, eye, eye!"

What happened to the man who didn't pay his exorcist?

He got re-possessed!

Did you hear about the monster who was a Star Trek fan?

He had one right ear, one left ear, and one final front-ear!

Why are ghost kids so happy at the end of the week?

It's Fright Day!

What happened when the vampire bit the cupcake?

She got frostingbite!

What do ghosts use to wash their hair?
Shamboo.

Why did the scarecrow win the Nobel Prize?
He was outstanding in his field!

Who is the scariest singer on the planet?
The Grim Rapper.

That was
a horrible
mummy joke!

I'll say.
It sphinx!

Why did it take so long for Godzilla to gobble up the tower of Big Ben?
It was time-consuming!

What do you call a hairy monster flying a helicopter?
A whirr-wolf!

Why did the zombie get a massage?
She was a little stiff!

SHAGGY: Poor Scooby! The police put him in jail after he ran away from the slime monster.
FRED: Why?
SHAGGY: **He was arrested for leaving the scene of the grime!**

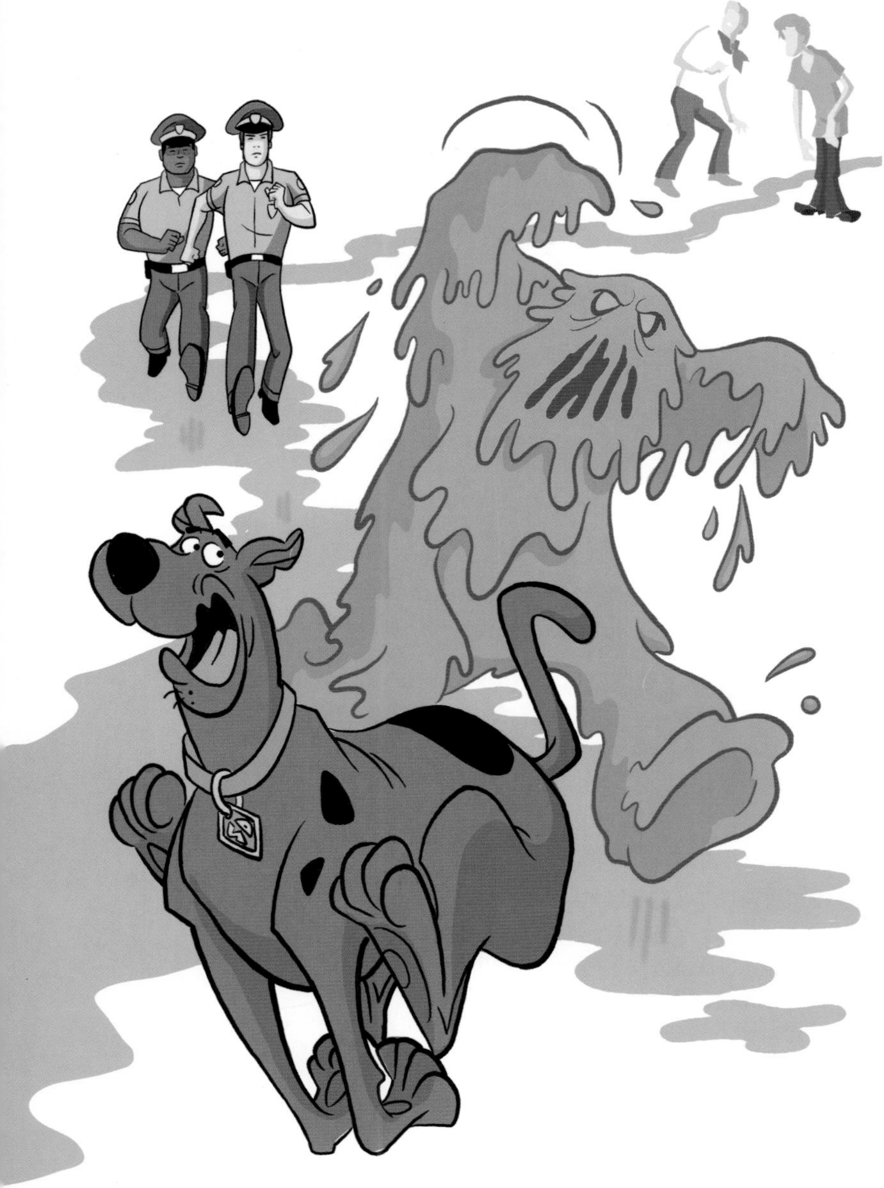

How to Tell Jokes!

1. KNOW the joke.

Make sure you remember the whole joke before you tell it. This sounds like a no-brainer, but most of us have known someone who says, "Oh, this is so funny . . ." Then, when they tell the joke, they can't remember the end. And that's the whole point of a joke – its punch line.

2. SPEAK CLEARLY.

Don't mumble; don't speak too fast or too slow. Just speak like you normally do. You don't have to use a different voice or accent or sound like someone else. (UNLESS that's part of the joke!)

3. LOOK at your audience.

Good eye contact with your listeners will grab their attention.

4. DON'T WORRY about gestures or how to stand or sit when you tell your joke. Remember, telling a joke is basically talking.

5. DON'T LAUGH at your own joke.

Yeah, yeah, I know some comedians break up while they're acting in a sketch or telling a story, but the best rule to follow is not to laugh. If you start to laugh, you might lose the rhythm of your joke or keep yourself from telling the joke clearly. Let your audience laugh. That's their job. Your job is to be the funny one.

6. THE PUNCH LINE is the most important part of the joke.

It's the climax, the payoff, the main event. A good joke can sound even better if you pause for just a second or two before you deliver the punch line. That tiny pause will make your audience mentally sit up and hold their breath, eager to hear what's coming next.

7. The SETUP is the second most important part of a joke.

That's basically everything you say before you get to the punch line. And that's why you need to be as clear as you can (see 2 above) so that when you finally reach the punch line, it makes sense!

8. YOU CAN GET FUNNIER.

It's easy. Watch other comedians. Listen to other people tell a joke or story. Check out a good comedy show or film. You can pick up some skills simply by seeing how others get their comedy across. You will absorb it! And soon it will come naturally.

9. Last, but not least, telling a joke is all about TIMING.

That means not only getting the biggest impact for your joke, waiting for the right time, giving that extra pause before the punch line — but it also means knowing when NOT to tell a joke. When you're among friends, you can tell when they'd like to hear something funny. But in an unfamiliar setting, get a "sense of the room" first. Are people having a good time? Or is it a more serious event? A joke has the most funny power when it's told in the right setting.

Michael Dahl

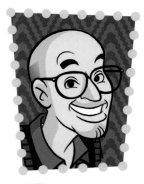

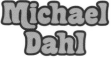

How is **Michael Dahl** like a vampire at the library?

They both want a good book they can sink their teeth into!

When Dahl is not reading good books, he's writing them. He has penned more than two hundred books for young readers. He is the author of *The Everything Kids' Joke Book*, *Laff-O-Tronic Joke Books*, the scintillating *Duck Goes Potty*, and two humorous mystery series: Finnegan Zwake (a "wisecracking riot" according to the *Chicago Tribune*) and Hocus Pocus Hotel. He toured the country with an improv troupe and began his auspicious comic career in fifth grade when his stand-up routine made his music teacher laugh so hard she fell off her chair. She is not available for comment.

Scott Jeralds

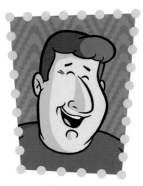

Why did the Abominable Snowman have **Scott Jeralds** draw his portrait?

Because he's a cool artist!

Jeralds has worked in animation for companies including Marvel Studios, Hanna-Barbera Studios, M.G.M. Animation, Warner Bros., and Porchlight Entertainment. Scott has worked on TV series such as *The Flintstones*, *Yogi Bear*, *Scooby-Doo*, *The Jetsons*, *Krypto the Superdog*, *Tom and Jerry*, *The Pink Panther*, *Superman*, *Secret Saturdays*, and he directed the cartoon series *Freakazoid*, for which he earned an Emmy Award. In addition, Scott has designed cartoon-related merchandise, licensing art, and artwork for several comic and children's book publications.

Joke Dictionary!

bit (BIT)—a section of a comedy routine

comedian (kuh-MEE-dee-uhn)—an entertainer who makes people laugh

headliner (HED-lye-ner)—the last comedian to perform in a show

improvisation (im-PRAH-vuh-ZAY-shuhn)—a performance that hasn't been planned: "improv" for short

lineup (LINE-uhp)—a list of people who are going to perform in a show

one-liner (WUHN-lye-ner)—a short joke or funny remark

open mike (OH-puhn MIKE)—an event at which anyone can use the microphone to perform for the audience

punch line (PUHNCH line)—the words at the end of a joke that make it funny or surprising

shtick (SHTIK)—a repetitive, comic performance or routine

segue (SEG-way)—a sentence or phrase that leads from one joke or routine to another

stand-up (STAND-uhp)—the type of comedy performed while standing alone on stage

timing (TIME-ing)—the use of rhythm and tempo to make a joke funnier

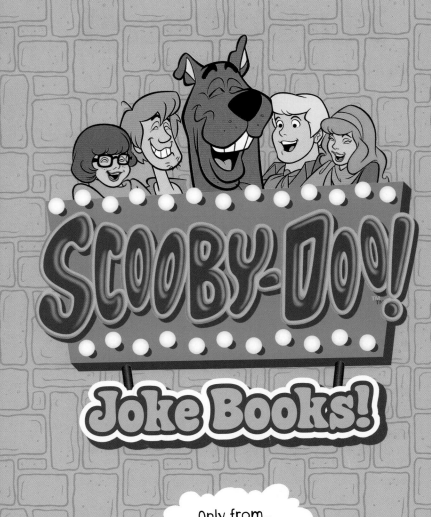

Only from...
STONE ARCH BOOKS!

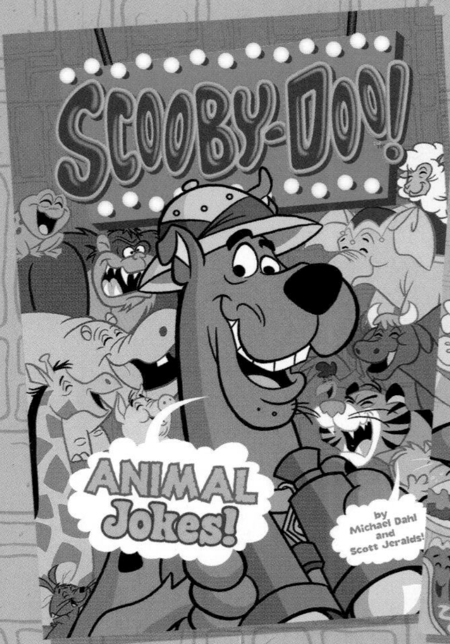
SCOOBY-DOO!
ANIMAL Jokes!
by
Michael Dahl
and
Scott Jeralds!

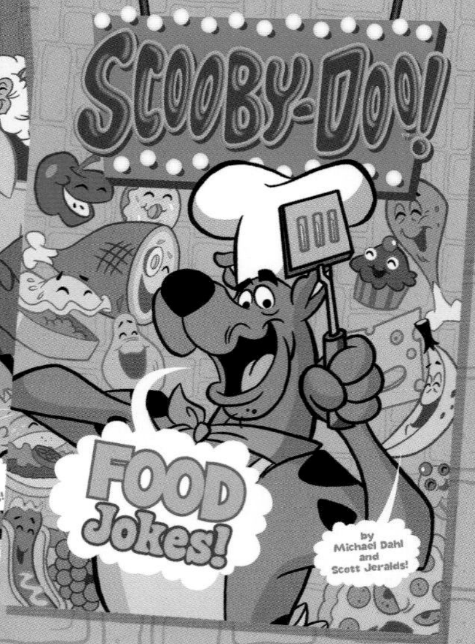
SCOOBY-DOO!
FOOD Jokes!
by
Michael Dahl
and
Scott Jeralds!

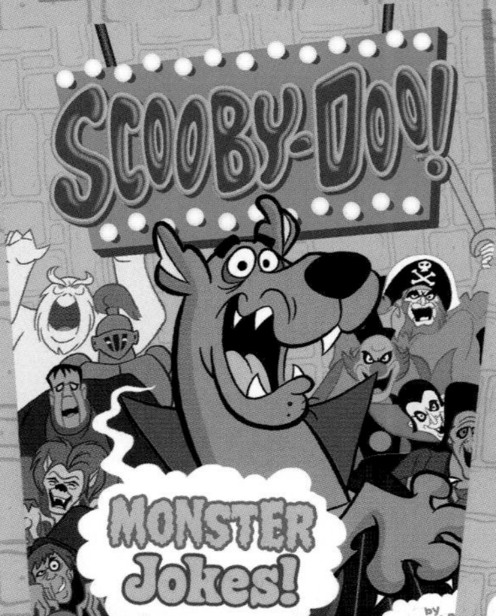
SCOOBY-DOO!
MONSTER Jokes!
by
and

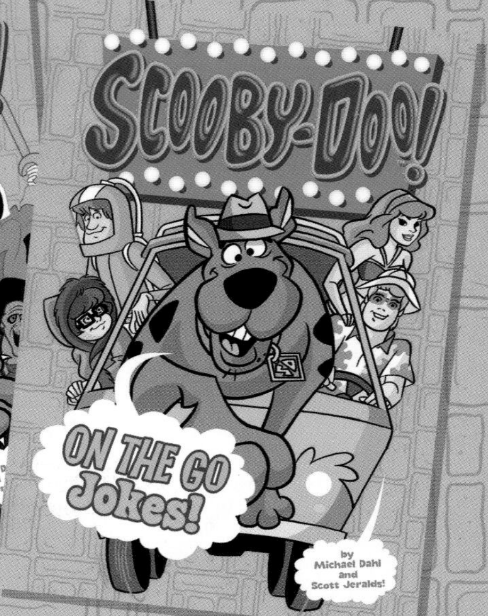
SCOOBY-DOO!
ON THE GO Jokes!
by
Michael Dahl
and
Scott Jeralds!

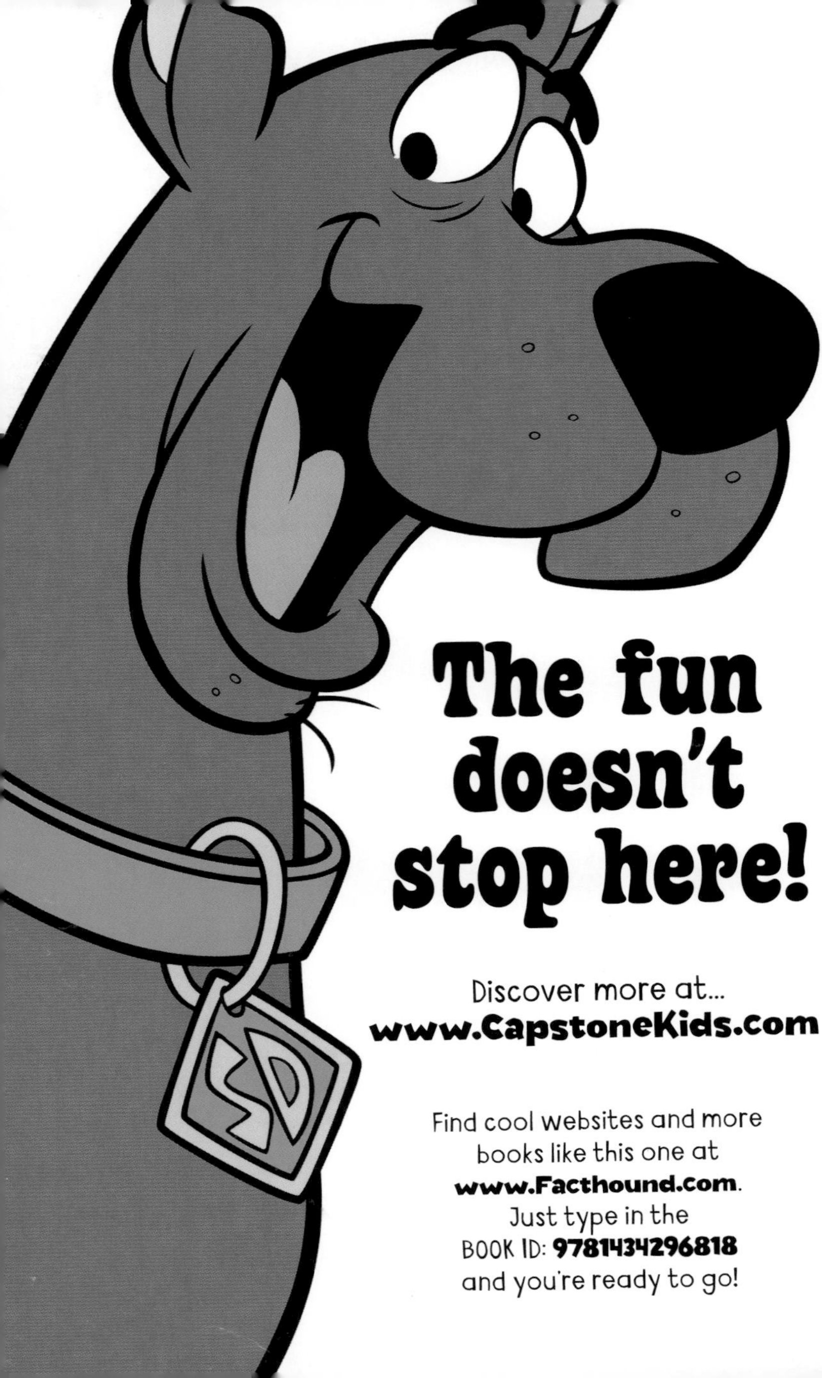

The fun doesn't stop here!

Discover more at...
www.CapstoneKids.com

Find cool websites and more books like this one at **www.Facthound.com**. Just type in the BOOK ID: **9781434296818** and you're ready to go!